This Journal Belongs To:

_____

A message For You!

Hello, how are you today? What made you smile today?
I just wanted to check on you and let you know that you are AMAZING!

This journal was designed to help you express and acknowledge your feelings and thoughts. You are destined for greatness and can do anything that you put your mind to.

Each day:
- Say the Affirmations out loud
- Choose how you are feeling
- Write down what you are grateful for
- Reflect on your day
- Spend time doodling to get your creative juices flowing.

I hope you enjoy this journal.

-Jamarion

7 Rules of Life

LET IT GO
Never ruin a good day by thinking about a bad yesterday.

IGNORE THEM
Don't listen to other people tell you what you cannot do. Live a life that's empowering to you.

GIVE IT TIME
Nothing good comes easy. Stay consistent and be determined.

DONT COMPARE
The only person you should try to beat is the person you were yesterday.

STAY CALM
It's ok to not have everything figured out. In time you'll get there.

IT'S ON YOU
Only you are in charge of your happiness.

SMILE
Enjoy every minute of each day. Find a reason to smile.

Do you know how AWESOME you are?

Do you know
that you were BORN to do
GREAT things?

Do you know
how much you are LOVED?

You are a GIFT to this world...

Let's Start Journaling

Today's date is

Today's Affirmation
"I AM ENOUGH"

How I'm Feeling

I am / I can / I will...

_____

Today I Am Grateful For...

1._____

2._____

3._____

What made you smile today ?

_____

_____

Reflection

How was your day overall?

_____

_____

_____

_____

_____

_____

_____

Doodles

Today's date is

Today's Affirmation
"I AM BRAVE"

How I'm Feeling

:) :(:| >:(

I am / I can / I will...

_____

Today I Am Grateful For...

1. _____

2. _____

3. _____

what made you smile today ?

_____

_____

Reflection

How was your day overall?

_____

_____

_____

_____

_____

_____

_____

Doodles

Today's date is

Today's Affirmation
"I CAN DO GREAT THNIGS"

How I'm Feeling

I am / I can / I will...

_____

Today I Am Grateful For...

1. _____

2. _____

3. _____

what made you smile today ?

_____

_____

Reflection

How was your day overall?

_____

_____

_____

_____

_____

_____

_____

Doodles

Today's date is

Today's Affirmation
"I MATTER"

How I'm Feeling

😊 😔 😐 😠

I am / I can / I will...

_____

Today I Am Grateful For...

1. _____

2. _____

3. _____

What made you smile today ?

_____

_____

Reflection

How was your day overall?

_____

_____

_____

_____

_____

_____

_____

Doodles

Today's date is

_____

Today's Affirmation
"I AM A LEADER"

How I'm Feeling

☺ ☹ 😐 😠

I am / I can / I will...

_____

Today I Am Grateful For...

1. _____

2. _____

3. _____

What made you smile today ?

_____

_____

Reflection

How was your day overall?

_____

_____

_____

_____

_____

_____

_____

Doodles

List 3 things that you do well!

_____

_____

_____

YOU CAN DO HARD THINGS!

Today's date is

Today's Affirmation
"I MAKE A DIFFERENCE"

How I'm Feeling

I am / I can / I will...

_____

Today I Am Grateful For...

1._____

2._____

3._____

what made you smile today ?

_____

_____

Reflection

How was your day overall?

_____

_____

_____

_____

_____

_____

_____

Doodles

Today's date is

_____

Today's Affirmation
"I AM SMART"

How I'm Feeling

😊 😞 😐 😠

I am / I can / I will...

_____

Today I Am Grateful For...

1. _____

2. _____

3. _____

What made you smile today ?

_____

_____

Reflection

How was your day overall?

_____

_____

_____

_____

_____

_____

_____

Doodles

Today's date is

Today's Affirmation
"I AM ROYAL"

How I'm Feeling

I am / I can / I will...

_____

Today I Am Grateful For...

1. _____

2. _____

3. _____

What made you smile today ?

_____

_____

Reflection

How was your day overall?

_____

_____

_____

_____

_____

_____

_____

Doodles

Today's date is

Today's Affirmation
"I AM A HIGH ACHIEVER"

How I'm Feeling

I am / I can / I will...

_____

Today I Am Grateful For...

1. _____

2. _____

3. _____

what made you smile today ?

_____

_____

Reflection

How was your day overall?

_____

_____

_____

_____

_____

_____

_____

Doodles

Today's date is

Today's Affirmation
"I AM A WINNER"

How I'm Feeling

😊 😞 😐 😠

I am / I can / I will...

_____

Today I Am Grateful For...

1._____

2._____

3._____

what made you smile today ?

_____

_____

Reflection

How was your day overall?

_____

_____

_____

_____

_____

_____

_____

Doodles

Write a Reminder to Yourself!

I AM......

_____

_____

_____

_____

_____

_____

_____

_____

LOVE YOURSELF

Today's date is

Today's Affirmation
"I AM COURAGEOUS"

How I'm Feeling

I am / I can / I will...

_____

Today I Am Grateful For...

1. _____

2. _____

3. _____

What made you smile today ?

_____

_____

Reflection

How was your day overall?

_____

_____

_____

_____

_____

_____

_____

 Doodles

Today's date is

Today's Affirmation
"I AM LOVED"

How I'm Feeling

I am / I can / I will...

_____

Today I Am Grateful For...

1._____

2._____

3._____

What made you smile today ?

_____

_____

Reflection

How was your day overall?

_____

_____

_____

_____

_____

_____

_____

Doodles

Today's date is

Today's Affirmation
"I AM CLEVER"

How I'm Feeling

😊 ☹️ 😐 😠

I am / I can / I will...

_____

Today I Am Grateful For...

1. _____

2. _____

3. _____

What made you smile today ?

_____

_____

Reflection

How was your day overall?

_____

_____

_____

_____

_____

_____

_____

Doodles

Today's date is

Today's Affirmation
"I WILL DO GREAT THINGS"

How I'm Feeling

😊 😣 😐 😠

I am / I can / I will...

_____

Today I Am Grateful For...

1. _____

2. _____

3. _____

what made you smile today ?

_____

_____

Reflection

How was your day overall?

_____

_____

_____

_____

_____

_____

_____

Doodles

Today's date is

Today's Affirmation
"I AM DESTINED FOR GREATNESS"

How I'm Feeling

I am / I can / I will...

_____

Today I Am Grateful For...

1._____

2._____

3._____

what made you smile today ?

_____

_____

Reflection

How was your day overall?

_____

_____

_____

_____

_____

_____

_____

Doodles

Level Up
write 3 areas of growth.
(Example: I want to read more.)

GROW THROUGH WHAT YOU GO THROUGH

Today's date is

Today's Affirmation
"I BELIEVE IN ME"

How I'm Feeling

I am / I can / I will...

_____

Today I Am Grateful For...

1. _____

2. _____

3. _____

What made you smile today ?

_____

_____

Reflection

How was your day overall?

_____

_____

_____

_____

_____

_____

_____

Doodles

Today's date is

Today's Affirmation
"I MAY MAKE MISTAKES, AND THAT'S OK"

How I'm Feeling

I am / I can / I will...

_____

Today I Am Grateful For...

1. _____

2. _____

3. _____

What made you smile today?

_____

_____

Reflection

How was your day overall?

_____

_____

_____

_____

_____

_____

_____

Doodles

Today's date is

Today's Affirmation
"I HAVE A PURPOSE"

How I'm Feeling

I am / I can / I will...

_____

Today I Am Grateful For...

1._____

2._____

3._____

What made you smile today ?

_____

_____

Reflection

How was your day overall?

_____

_____

_____

_____

_____

_____

_____

Doodles

Today's date is

_____

Today's Affirmation
"I AM MAGNIFICENT"

How I'm Feeling

😊 😞 😐 😠

I am / I can / I will...

_____

Today I Am Grateful For...

1. _____

2. _____

3. _____

What made you smile today ?

_____

_____

Reflection

How was your day overall?

_____

_____

_____

_____

_____

_____

_____

Doodles

Today's date is

Today's Affirmation
"I AM ONE OF A KIND"

How I'm Feeling

😊 😔 😐 😠

I am / I can / I will...

_____

Today I Am Grateful For...

1. _____

2. _____

3. _____

what made you smile today ?

_____

_____

Reflection

How was your day overall?

_____

_____

_____

_____

_____

_____

_____

Doodles

Listen to your heart!

what are 3 songs that help you deal with your feelings?

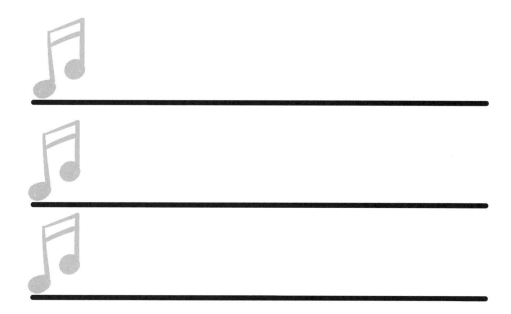

CHASE YOUR DREAMS

Today's date is

Today's Affirmation
"I AM IMPORTANT"

How I'm Feeling

😊 😞 😐 😠

I am / I can / I will...

_____

Today I Am Grateful For...

1. _____

2. _____

3. _____

What made you smile today ?

_____

_____

Reflection

How was your day overall?

_____

_____

_____

_____

_____

_____

_____

Doodles

Today's date is

Today's Affirmation
"I CAN DO HARD THINGS"

How I'm Feeling

I am / I can / I will...

_____

Today I Am Grateful For...

1._____

2._____

3._____

What made you smile today ?

_____

_____

Reflection

How was your day overall?

_____

_____

_____

_____

_____

_____

_____

Doodles

Today's date is

Today's Affirmation
"I FOCUS ON THE GOOD"

How I'm Feeling
☺ ☹ 😐 😠

I am / I can / I will...

_____

Today I Am Grateful For...

1._____

2._____

3._____

what made you smile today ?

_____

_____

Reflection

How was your day overall?

_____

_____

_____

_____

_____

_____

_____

Doodles

Today's date is

Today's Affirmation
"I WILL BE WEALTHY"

How I'm Feeling

I am / I can / I will...

_____

Today I Am Grateful For...

1. _____

2. _____

3. _____

What made you smile today ?

_____

_____

Reflection

How was your day overall?

_____

_____

_____

_____

_____

_____

_____

Doodles

Today's date is

___

Today's Affirmation
"I CALM AND PEACEFUL"

How I'm Feeling
😊 ☹️ 😐 😠

I am / I can / I will...

_____

Today I Am Grateful For...

1. _____

2. _____

3. _____

What made you smile today ?

_____

_____

Reflection

How was your day overall?

_____

_____

_____

_____

_____

_____

_____

Doodles

Design your
Ultimate Motivational Tee

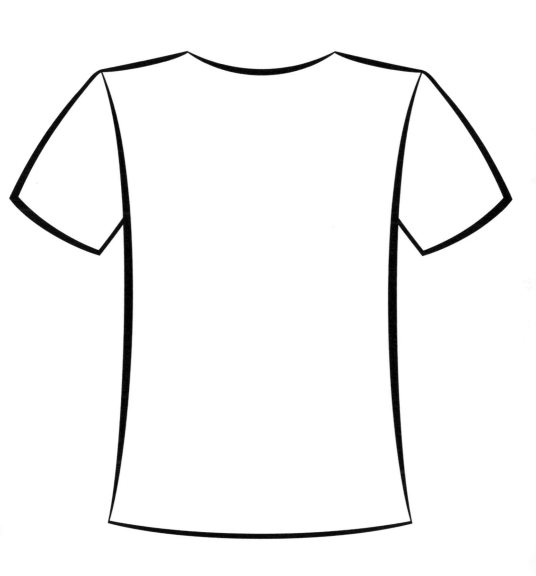

YOU ARE THE ARTIST OF YOUR MASTERPIECE

Today's date is

Today's Affirmation
"I AM JOVIAL"

How I'm Feeling

:) :(:| >:(

I am / I can / I will...

_____

Today I Am Grateful For...

1. _____

2. _____

3. _____

What made you smile today ?

_____

_____

Reflection

How was your day overall?

_____

_____

_____

_____

_____

_____

_____

Doodles

Today's date is

Today's Affirmation
"I AM HILARIOUS"

How I'm Feeling

I am / I can / I will...

_____

Today I Am Grateful For...

1._____

2._____

3._____

what made you smile today ?

_____

_____

Reflection

How was your day overall?

_____

_____

_____

_____

_____

_____

_____

Doodles

Today's date is

Today's Affirmation
"I AM WORTHY OF GOOD THINGS"

How I'm Feeling

I am / I can / I will...

_____

Today I Am Grateful For...

1. _____

2. _____

3. _____

What made you smile today ?

_____

_____

Reflection

How was your day overall?

_____

_____

_____

_____

_____

_____

_____

Doodles

Today's date is

Today's Affirmation
"I BELIEVE IN MYSELF"

How I'm Feeling

I am / I can / I will...

_____

Today I Am Grateful For...

1. _____

2. _____

3. _____

What made you smile today ?

_____

_____

Reflection

How was your day overall?

_____

_____

_____

_____

_____

_____

_____

Doodles

Today's date is

Today's Affirmation
"I DESERVE SELF-RESPECT"

How I'm Feeling

😊 😞 😐 😠

I am / I can / I will...

_____

Today I Am Grateful For...

1._____

2._____

3._____

What made you smile today ?

_____

_____

Reflection

How was your day overall?

_____

_____

_____

_____

_____

_____

_____

Doodles

Today's date is

Today's Affirmation
"I AM UNSTOPPABLE"

How I'm Feeling

I am / I can / I will...

_____

Today I Am Grateful For...

1. _____

2. _____

3. _____

what made you smile today ?

_____

_____

Reflection

How was your day overall?

_____

_____

_____

_____

_____

_____

_____

Doodles

Today's date is

Today's Affirmation
"I LOVE MYSELF FULLY"

How I'm Feeling

I am / I can / I will...

_____

Today I Am Grateful For...

1._____

2._____

3._____

What made you smile today ?

_____

_____

Reflection

How was your day overall?

_____

_____

_____

_____

_____

_____

_____

Doodles

Today's date is

Today's Affirmation
"I RADIATE POSITIVITY"

How I'm Feeling

I am / I can / I will...

_____

Today I Am Grateful For...

1. _____

2. _____

3. _____

What made you smile today?

_____

_____

Reflection

How was your day overall?

_____

_____

_____

_____

_____

_____

_____

Doodles

Today's date is

Today's Affirmation
"MY MISTAKES HELP ME GROW"

How I'm Feeling

😊 😟 😐 😠

I am / I can / I will...

_____

Today I Am Grateful For...

1._____

2._____

3._____

What made you smile today ?

_____

_____

Reflection

How was your day overall?

_____

_____

_____

_____

_____

_____

_____

Doodles

Today's date is

Today's Affirmation
"I CAN ACHIEVE ANYTHING"

How I'm Feeling

☺ ☹ 😐 😠

I am / I can / I will...

_____

Today I Am Grateful For...

1. _____

2. _____

3. _____

What made you smile today?

_____

_____

Reflection

How was your day overall?

_____

_____

_____

_____

_____

_____

_____

 Doodles

Today's date is

Today's Affirmation
"I MAKE A DIFFERENCE"

How I'm Feeling

😊 😞 😐 😠

I am / I can / I will...

_____

Today I Am Grateful For...

1._____

2._____

3._____

What made you smile today ?

_____

_____

Reflection

How was your day overall?

_____

_____

_____

_____

_____

_____

_____

Doodles

You Did It!

You've gotten through the entire Gratitude Journal.

You have taken the time to express your *feelings* and understand your thoughts.

I hope that you are happier, more brave, more confident and ready to take on the world being the best you that you can be.
You are MAGICAL in every way!

I'm so proud of YOU!

Thoughts

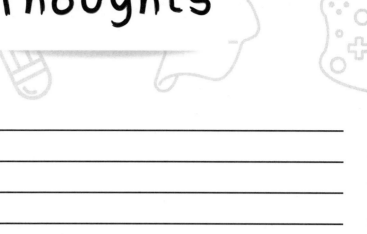

_____
_____
_____
_____
_____
_____
_____
_____
_____
_____
_____
_____
_____
_____
_____
_____

Thoughts

Thoughts

Thoughts

Thoughts

Thoughts

Get to know
JAMARION

Jamarion is a 15-year old entrepreneur who loves graphic design, food, music, games and basketball. After he began writing down his feelings, he noticed that journaling changed how he felt each day.

He wanted a way to bring awareness to mental health and help other young boys learn to express their feelings.
This journal is just the beginning of his journey to spread joy and positivity.

Want to share your Journaling fun?

Tag Jamarion on social media:
@brwnpaperco

Use Hashtag:
#JournalWithJam